Crossing the Sea

過 海

DuoDuo

多 多

Edited by Lee Robinson
Translated by Lee Robinson and Yu Li Ming
Afterword by Nino Ricci

Poems copyright © 1998 by DuoDuo
Translation copyright © 1998 by Lee Robinson
Afterword copyright © 1998 by Nino Ricci

Published in 1998 by
House of Anansi Press Limited
1800 Steeles Avenue West, Concord, ON
Canada L4K 2P3

Distributed in Canada by
General Distribution Services Inc.
30 Lesmill Road
Toronto, Canada M3B 2T6
Tel. (416) 445-3333
Fax (416) 445-5967
e-mail: Customer.Service@ccmailgw.genpub.com

02 01 00 99 98   1 2 3 4 5

Canadian Cataloguing in Publication Data
DuoDuo, 1951-
DuoDuo: crossing the sea ; poems in exile/poems in China
Translated from Chinese.
ISBN 0-88784-562-2

I. DuoDuo, 1951- . Translations into English. I. Robinson, Lee, 1959-
II. Yu, Li Ming, 1945- . III. Title. IV. Title: Crossing the sea.
PL2910.Z65D86 1998   895.1'.152   C95-930336-7

Cover Illustration: DuoDuo, *Untitled*, oil on canvas, 1993
Cover Photograph: Arjan Roos, Rotterdam
Author Photograph: Ekko von Schwichow, Berlin
Printed and bound in Canada
Typesetting: ECW Type & Art, Oakville

*House of Anansi Press gratefully acknowledges the
Canada Council for the Arts and the Ontario Arts Council
for their support of our publishing program.*

Crossing the Sea

CONTENTS

Poems in China

NOTE ON THE EDITION AND TRANSLATION

This project was initiated by author and columnist John Fraser, formerly the *Globe and Mail's* correspondent from China, who had befriended DuoDuo and believed there should be a Canadian book of his poetry that would include work he had done since his exile in 1989. This book began with a body of forty-four poems translated by Huainian Hu. At DuoDuo's request I then became involved as editor and brought in Yu Li Ming, who translated a larger body of poems. Then began a lengthy process of collaboration between Yu Li Ming and myself. We spent many hours poring over the Chinese originals and the literal translations, discovering in DuoDuo's poetry a syntax often complex, rebellious, and ironic, and a content that ranged from the humorous to the heartfelt to the surreal.

DuoDuo's poems, short stories, essays, and plays are now variously available in Dutch, German, Italian, Japanese, and English. I should note that DuoDuo's name is generally translated as two words, "Duo Duo," in the United States, as well as in Germany and Italy, and as one word, spelled "Duoduo," in the U.K. and the Netherlands. The name in Chinese is a single character repeated twice, meaning literally "much much." DuoDuo took this pen name from the name of his daughter, who died in infancy in 1982.

The selection in this book was chosen from an oeuvre of over 150 poems provided by the poet. DuoDuo was available for consultation throughout the editing and translation process, at times in person in Canada and at other times long-distance from Europe. Almost all the Poems in Exile have been published in Chinese in the new *Today*, the renowned Chinese literary journal reestablished outside China in 1990. Of the Poems in China, most can be found in DuoDuo's two books published there: his official book, *Salute: 38 Poems* (1988), and his more comprehensive, unofficial book, *Milestones: Selected Poems 1972–1988* (1989). Eleven of the Poems in China are not included in either of his Chinese books.

As words in poems mean not so much their denotations as their usage in the living language, translation often required much discussion between Yu Li Ming and myself. For example, the short early poem "Dusk" contains the image of a sleepless poet "in a dusk sabotaged as usual/by servants"; yet in 1973 China, no one, including DuoDuo's family, had household servants. When I asked Li Ming how the word "servant" might occur in the language at that time, he instantly replied with the commonplace Communist expression "the people's servants." DuoDuo was using "servants" as shorthand, which would have been obvious to Chinese readers; we have translated "people's servants" for our Western readers. In this manner of inquiry about particular words and phrases, I learned from Li Ming a great deal about Chinese history and culture.

Li Ming and I were fortunate in being able to consult quite a number of other English translations of some of the poems in this book, which provided much insight and guidance. These translators are: Gregory Lee, John Cayley, Maghiel van Crevel, Jin Zhong sometimes with Steven Haven, Donald Finkel, Tang Chao, and Michelle Yeh. Other translators from whom we saw only one poem each are: Tony Barnstone with Newton Liu, John Rosenwald, and Yun Wang. I wish to fully acknowledge our indebtedness to these translators, especially to Gregory Lee, who, with John Cayley, translated DuoDuo's two existing books of poetry in English, both out of the U.K.: *Statements: The New Chinese Poetry of Duoduo* (Wellsweep, 1989), which was then revised and expanded as *Looking out from Death: From the Cultural Revolution to Tiananmen Square* (Bloomsbury, 1989).

These publications coincided with the moment of DuoDuo's exile — his fateful trip to England on June 4, 1989; ours is the first English book of DuoDuo's poems to contain his work in exile. It is worth noting that the British books were both rushed into print, whereas Li Ming and I have worked at length together as a native Chinese and a native English speaker, and so it has been possible for us to correct, I believe, some errors of translation which inevitably occurred in the prior books, and have occurred also in other translations.

Of the Poems in Exile contained here, nine have previously appeared in book form in English only in Maghiel van Crevel's PhD thesis on DuoDuo, published in the Netherlands in 1996 as *Language Shattered: Contemporary Chinese Poetry and Duoduo*. One of the Poems in Exile was included in *New Tide: Contemporary Chinese Poetry*, a bilingual, English/Chinese anthology published in Canada in 1992, on which I served in an editorial role. The remaining twelve Poems in Exile have never before been available in book form in English, and seven are translated to English for the first time herein.

Of the Poems in China, four poems, "Poet," "At Fifteen," "Characters," and "It's," as well as part F of "*from* Winter Night Woman," are only otherwise available in book form in English in Maghiel van Crevel's book out of the Netherlands. Three further Poems in China, including the long poem "One Story Tells His Entire Past," have never before been published in book form in English, and two of these — the long early poem, "Honeyweek," and "30 June 1986" — are translated to English for the first time herein. In the case of "*from* Winter Night Woman," parts A and B have never before been translated to English, and part E has formerly been available in English only in mimeograph within China. The remaining Poems in China are variously published in book form in English in DuoDuo's two previous collections of poetry out of the U.K., as well as in three translated anthologies of contemporary Chinese poetry out of the United States, and the one bilingual anthology out of Canada.

I have also been very fortunate in my editors, the Canadian poets Steven Heighton and Victor Coleman, who worked very hard, often seeing the same poem more than once. My work on this book has transpired over a period of five years, and though it now seems a long time ago, the fact is that when I first tackled the task of translation I was completely at sea, despite having just edited the anthology of contemporary Chinese poetry which included DuoDuo. Steven Heighton and Victor Coleman literally showed me the way, both in their edits and in letters containing instruction, conjecture, opinion. Yet, once they had taught me to do my job, their input became no less illuminating.

The fact that they have two very different styles of editing was a great benefit: Steven enjoining me to open up the poems, and Victor to pare down. Steven saw more poems and gave a greater volume of comments, addressing the demands of each individual poem, while Victor worked towards a consistent overall poetics. Both editors have authored lines in this book, especially Steven, and the book you hold in your hands wouldn't have been possible without both of them. These English-language poets have helped us to produce, I believe, not only the most error-free but also the most poetically worthy English translation of DuoDuo's poems yet to exist.

DuoDuo's poems in the original Chinese are sparsely punctuated and typically conclude with an ellipsis. We've translated to full punctuation and have eliminated the closing ellipses. Also, DuoDuo often uses commas after noun phrases and before a verb — part, I would argue, of his commitment to a poetics of the emphatic — which is idiosyncratic in Chinese, but anathema in English. We've allowed one to survive, in the closing line of "Handicraft": "She, is my wasted days."

Chinese characters are not conjugated; thus, there are no verb tenses. We've preferred the present tense, and often found that utilizing a verb tense allowed us to eliminate certain modifying words, such as "just," "already," "starts to," and "continues to." Chinese characters also don't take on plural forms. While occasionally a noun is marked as one or many by modifying characters, largely decisions as to whether each noun is singular or plural had to be made in the context of the poem, and many could be reinterpreted.

English translates about thirty percent longer than the original Chinese. Thus, poems sometimes had to be cut down to maintain their original structure, or, more often, the structure had to be enlarged to contain its content. In some cases, such as "Silkworm: Textile," every single line of the Chinese became two English lines. "September," a poem originally all three-line stanzas, became all four-line stanzas. "Reading Out Loud" was maintained as all three-line stanzas, but one stanza was added. In all cases, an effort was made to respect the integrity of the original poem.

However, some liberties have been taken. We omitted two closing stanzas from "Never Make Dreams," and changed the title of the poem "Winter Day" to "Reading Out Loud." In "Watching the Sea," DuoDuo repeats the single word "surely" over and over, whereas we have substituted numerous synonyms. I take the titles for the two sections of short, early poems, "Thoughts and Recollections" and "Everything under the Sun," from DuoDuo's book *Milestones*, but I have rearranged and added to the poems included under those titles. In the poem "At Fifteen," I've added the epigraph from Confucius because this allusion would likely be apparent to Chinese readers, but lost on Westerners. The translation of Confucius has been extrapolated from translations by Ezra Pound and William Edward Soothill. It is useful to note that DuoDuo turned fifteen the year the Cultural Revolution erupted, in 1966.

In the early poems, written during or shortly after the Cultural Revolution (1966–76), the images of the sun and sunflowers and the east have a significance that's difficult for Western readers to comprehend. The language of the Revolution was saturated with metaphors of Mao as sun. Two constantly repeated slogans, often printed boxed in newspapers, were: "Chairman Mao is the never-setting sun" and "Chairman Mao is the reddest red sun in our hearts." One frequently sung song began with the lines "O, Chairman Mao, / You are the radiant sun. / We are sunflowers. / Nourished by your sunshine/We grow vigorously." The Communist Party song "East is Red," which came to be regarded as equally sacred as the national anthem, opens with the lines, "Red is east. / Rises the sun. / China has brought forth/A Mao Tse-tung."

A few more specific notes on the poems that might be helpful to Western readers: the political connotations of left and right in these poems are opposite to ours; left as communist is establishment, mainstream, official culture, while right as pro-democracy is dissident, radical, underground culture. The "duck-tongue cap" in "Honey-week" is the literal Chinese name for what we would simply call a cap. In "Silkworm: Textile," it is helpful to know that silkworms actually kill themselves in producing silk: they empty the contents of their heads as silk cocoons. The sections of the poems "Gallery" and *"from* Winter Night Woman" in the original Chinese were headed with letters from the Roman alphabet, no doubt a nod to the Western poetry DuoDuo was reading. In "One Story Tells His Entire Past," the phrase "cow pen" refers to rudimentary prison cells used during the Cultural Revolution. The poem "Characters" is about writers submitting to censorship of the media. The *"mu"* in "Northern Earth" is the standard measure for land in China, equal to about one-sixteenth of an acre.

The hero of the poem "My Uncle" is the reformist (or at least so-called) Deng Xiaoping, China's "General Architect," who rose to power after the death of Mao in 1976 and died last year. The "bull" in the third line is Mao. The image of splicing "the sun back in history" alludes to the Communist Party habit of altering photographs to include or eliminate people whose political stars had risen or fallen, thus attempting to rewrite history. The architect striding "down the steps of his own design" is a pun on the many, multi-step directives issued by Deng. The "red tie" in the second last line refers to the name and emblem of the group to which schoolchildren belonged during the revolution, the Red Ties.

The phrase "foolish melons" in "At Fifteen" is colloquial Chinese, while the description of the people as "nails" in "Map" is part of the Communist Party rhetoric. Another allusion to such rhetoric appears in the repeated phrase "in this weather," in the poem "In This Weather, Weather Is Meaningless." The phrase is similar to the English expression "in this climate" and is heavily employed by the Party in reference to the socioeconomic conditions of China, so that, for instance, a statement will be issued that such-and-such is not possible "in this weather."

To me the most interesting Chinese coinage I came across in this work was a set of characters that appeared in the title poem, "Crossing the Sea," which we translated as "afterworld." The characters literally denoted "that side," after the Chinese concept of "that sidedness," meaning "the other side of life." It is an expression singularly bereft of religious import, being strictly speculative and expository. "Afterworld" was the most secular English rendering I could come up with, yet even it is tinged with the postulates of faith.

There is the question of how faithful these translations are. While modifications to the structure of the poems were often necessary, and while we have used full punctuation in lieu of DuoDuo's sparse punctuation and have eliminated his frequent closing ellipses, these translations are otherwise very faithful. Of course, accuracy is itself a debatable goal in translation. For example, the title of the second section of short poems, "Everything under the Sun," would more accurately be translated as "A Myriad of Things." But since the phrase is a colloquial Chinese expression delineating the whole contents of the world, "Everything under the Sun" as an English colloquialism for the same seems more accurate at least in tone. The only distinct variance between DuoDuo's poems and our translations, I believe, is that DuoDuo, as part of his pursuit of an emphatic poetics, often repeats words or phrases within a poem. This tendency, without being eliminated, has been minimized in our translations, sometimes by substituting a synonymous word or phrase for a repeated one, and sometimes by removing a repetition.

This book was a highly collaborative effort. I remember the words of DuoDuo when I began: "My job was to make a good Chinese poem; your job is to make a good English poem." I only hope that, with the excellent help of others, I have succeeded in that task.

Lee Robinson, March 1998

POEMS IN EXILE

I'm Reading

In the November wheat fields I'm reading my father.
I'm reading his hair,
the colour of his tie, the creases of his trousers
and his hooves, tripped up in shoelaces
skating, while playing the violin,
his scrotum tight, his neck
from too much comprehension craning to the sky.
I read that my father is a big-eyed horse.

I read as far as my father leaving the herd
briefly, his coat hung from a young tree
with his socks, and appearing faintly in the crowd
those pallid buttocks, like a lady's
toilet soap dangling
in an oyster stripped of meat.
I read the scent of my father's hair lotion,
the smell of tobacco about him
and his tuberculosis
illuminating the left lung of a horse.
I read to where a boy's doubts
rise from an amber cornfield,
to where I'm of an age to understand
rain starts over the red roofs where grain is spread to dry
and the seeding season's plough drags four dead horse legs,
horse hide an open umbrella and horse teeth everywhere.
I read face after face that time's taken with it.
I read to where my father's personal history rots
softly underground, and the locusts on his body
have long survived on their own.

Like a white-haired barber embracing an aging persimmon tree,
I read to where my father returns me to a horse's belly
when I'm turning into a stone bench in the London fog
and glance past men on the bank-lined boulevard.

1991

Crossing the Sea

We cross the sea, and where
should that cursed river flow?

We look back, but
no one follows.

Is there no one at all
worth repeated resurrection?

Passengers on the boat stand wooden,
their loved ones breathe under distant waters.

Resolute bells chime
as confidence fades.

Trees on the far shore look like copulating people.
Replacing seashells, starfish, sea anemones,

syringes scattered on the beach, cotton swabs,
pubic hair — is this the afterworld?

So we turn our heads, like fruit swivelling round
and behind us — a tombstone

thrust into the high-school yard.
Only those women crying over their children by the sea

anticipate the length of this winter.
Without people dying, the river is endless.

1990

Amsterdam's River

November where the city enters night
there's only Amsterdam's river.

Abruptly the tangerines
on the trees of home
shudder in autumn winds.

I shut the windows — useless.
The river flows upstream, no use either.
The pearl-studded sun rises

to no avail.
Flocks of doves scatter like filings.
Streets cleared of boys appear broad and spacious.

After autumn rains,
those roofs crawling with snails —
my country

slowly sails past on Amsterdam's river.

1989

In England

After church spires and city chimneys sink beneath the horizon,
England's sky is gloomier than lovers' whispers.
Two blind accordion players, heads bowed, pass by.

Without farmers there would be no vespers.
Without gravestones, no declaimers.
Two rows of new-sown apple trees stab at my heart.

My wings brought me fame. England
made me reach the place where I am lost.
Memory sustains, but no longer digs furrows.

My address: shame. All England
and not a woman who can't kiss. All England
cannot contain my pride.

In the dirt under my nails I recognize
my homeland — mother
sealed neatly in a parcel, posted far away.

1989–90

Walk into Winter

The tread through leaves turns to rotten fruit-
stones that sting the eyes of passers-by.

On a house's red roof
where grain once dried

the glistening husks of insects,
heaped up as autumn's contents.

First blush of the season brushes off
a heavy woollen coat.

Fungus quitting decayed coffin boards
walks into winter.

The boy in sunshine grows ugly.
His marble parents sob aloud:

When water courses into the well,
ploughs are stilled in the fields.

When iron bends in the blacksmith's hands,
harvesters wield sickles toward themselves.

Mourners gather together
and stagger, drunk.

The translating flux of
May's wheat waves is far away.

Trees stare into the distance
that's ready to marry them off.

Cows resist the motion of the heavens
as if holding their pent up dung.

1989

Reading Out Loud

The last streak of light warms the church spire.
The stove fire in the church is out
for hours, days.

I look for what I've lost
and what I find, drop —
done with words on gravestones

I wander this wide
sky and earth, eternal parents.
Prayers from the heart rise.

Silence and what lies beyond sound
thaw into winter's chat.
Wind is a solitary rider.

Clouds are bunched up
laughing country brides.
December's mystical palpitations

are merely
a flare-up of old
reading out loud.

1990

Watching the Sea

Once you've watched the winter sea, what flows in the veins
is surely blood no more.
So when making love you might gaze at the sea.
Surely you're still waiting,
waiting for the sea breeze to blow once more for you.
That breeze bound to rise from the bed.

Those memories are clearly
illusions of oceans anchored in
the eyes of dead fish.
Fishermen are openly
engineers and dentists on vacation.
June cotton in the earth is
strictly cotton swabs.
Likely you're still in the fields
looking for things to worry about.
The trees you brush past plainly show
big lumps from being bumped into.
Your phenomenal bad mood no doubt
grants you a fate
unique in this crowd
because you're too fond of saying surely,
as Indian women will
surely expose their flesh at the waist.

Not far for sure from where you share rooms,
not far at all from Chinatown either,
there is assuredly a moon
bright as a mouthful of spit.
Naturally some say your health is
no longer important or even more pressing — surely
it stays on your mind
as that imperious cannon remains
on England's coast.

Watching the sea
has certainly used up your prime.
The galaxies left in your eyes
are turned to ash; that's clear.
The sea's dark shadows doubtless
slipped through the seabottom
into another land. At night when
death inevitably visits someone,
a certain person surely has to die.
Though a ring is always unwilling
to endure on the corpse, the hormone-
injected horse rump unfailingly
turns skittish. So
to make order in fact involves
flipping through everything randomly.
With the chain fallen off,
pedals really spin like flying.
Spring breezes are unquestionably
the green waist belts
worn by kidney stone sufferers.
The taxi driver's face
absolutely resembles stewed fruit.
That old chair when you return home is
youthful, surely; and no mistake.

1989–90

Map

At midnight someone outside lures you.
Cigarette ember, a squirming silkworm.
On the desk the water in the glass agitates.
Open the drawer: a forty-year-long
snowstorm rages.

A voice (whose voice?) asks, *Is the sky*
the map?
You know the shouter's black lips.
You peg him. It's
you. Your old self.
You recognize your head
being coughed out the hospital window into the

distant horizon — where blacksmith and nails
swing in sync.
People trying to
put out a fire
crowd on a postage stamp,
urgently pour out the vast ocean.
Some swimmers splash each other,
their flour-sack bathing-suits imprinted:
nails far from their motherland.

In a gust of pungent air you smell
the storm's foreboding.
You glide down the aisles of hanging hooks
and float out the butcher's back window.
Behind you one leg stays put
on the chopping board.
You recognize it as your leg
because you've taken that step.

1990

I've Always Delighted in a Shaft of Light in the Depth of Night

In the noise of wind and bells I await that light.
On a morning asleep until noon,
the last leaves hang dreamily.
Teeming leaves wedge into winter.
Fallen leaves hem in the trees.
Trees on the rim of the sloping town
gather the winds of four seasons —

Who causes the wind to be misread
as the centre of being lost.
What keeps me listening closely
to trees hindering the wind,
flattening it again into
the harvest season's five
pried-open fingers.

The wind's shadow grows new leaves
from the hands of the dead. Nails
pulled out by hand. By tools in hands
clenched. Like the shadow of a human
walked over by humans.
Spitting image of human, yet
spat on by humans. There it is,
driving the last glint of light from
the eyes of the dead
yet honing ever brighter
light that slashes through the forest.

Against the radiance of spring
I enter the pre-dawn sheen.
I notice the one tree that
hates and remembers me.
Under it, under that apple tree,
the table in my memory turns green.
The wonders of May, bones by wings

startled awake, unfurl towards me.
I turn around; grass sprouts over my back.
I'm awake, and the sky is moving.
Death inscribed on faces enters characters
lit up by stars accustomed to death.
Death projects into light,
making the lone church
the last pole to measure starlight,
making the left out, left over.

1991

Often

Often they occupy iron benches in the park,
as they often wear many garments.
There was once life in their houses.
This city is often dreamt by them;
so is this world.

Often they feel hungry
even as they read the newspapers.
The hunger in countries far away
makes them sure to put on weight,
though only an ache is gained, their lives
not changing because of it.
While they read the papers
the maps keep getting fatter.

They were lovers, wives, mothers.
They still are,
but no one wants to remember them. Even
the pillows they shared with others
forget them. So
they talk to themselves more and more
as if to God. So they turn
good-hearted; if they weren't before

they're ready to listen now — to anyone,
humans, beasts, or rivers. Often they feel
they are that harbour
the ships they're awaiting
are leaving or entering.
Likely they won't go to Africa.
They'll slump on that fixed iron bench
and the exiles facing them
will cover themselves with apple blossoms
and fall asleep, fall asleep and dream
as if their wombs were a church for tomorrow.

1992

Morning

Whether it's morning or whenever, it's morning.
You dream of waking, you're afraid to wake
so you say you're frightened of string, afraid of
the bird-like face of a woman. So you dream your father
speaking bird talk, drinking bird milk. You dream
your father is a celibate
and by chance, not in dream,
he bears you. You dream the dream your father dreamed.
You dream your father says, *This is a dream dreamed by a dead man.*

You don't believe, but you incline to believing,
this is dream, only dream, your dream.
Once, it was the handlebar of a certain bicycle
retaining the hand's grip. Now,
drooping down on your father's lower belly,
once a fetus refusing to be born,
now it's you climbing back to the handlebar.
You've dreamed all the details in your dream,
like your father's teeth lying on the ground, sparkling,
laughing at you. So you're not death itself,
merely an instance: you've dreamed of your dream's death.

1991

In This Weather,
Weather Is Meaningless

Land sprawls void of measure,
rail lines speed in no direction.
Rejected by a dreamed-out dream,
shut up in a shoebox, compelled
by a want of options, in the time
an insect takes to creep by,
those fearful of death lean heavier on dread.

> *In this weather, you're*
> *a break in the weather.*

Whatever you watch watches you.
Inhaling its exhalation, you're bored into.
Glancing at the change before daybreak,
you find reason
to turn into grass.
Running along lawns grown by people,
you forget everything.

> *In this weather, you won't*
> *stand by weather's side.*

Nor can you stand by faith — only on the side of fiction.
When horses' hooves no longer drum up dictionaries,
could your tongue spit hornets no more?
When wheat ripens in fable
then rots away, would you
eat up the last plum in the nightingale's song?
Swallow it. Then leave the sound of winter on the bough.

> *In this weather, only*
> *fiction furthers.*

1992

Boy Catching Hornets

In a time without wind, there are birds.
"Birds, but no mornings."

The boy catching hornets
enters the picture from the right.

The tree's chatter
gives way to a bird's.

"Young mother, your grass fields face me."
Three suns chase the bird.

"Young mother, the calf in your womb is stirring."
The world's darkest horse gallops by.

"Mother, the coffin is carried from the south."
The tree is measuring, measuring the boy's head.

The boy's cries are sealed in a pear.
Many others lie outside the frame.

The boy used to stand on his five feet,
but his feet are now sand.

The leaveless sapling weeps.
Then an overripe plum shouts, "*You. We.*"

1992

Together

The light is on.
We are together
in the half that's devoid
of light.
Our memory
is elsewhere
in that half the light
is too weak to reach.
We imagine it
from lack of imagination.
We are smoking.
Perhaps too early.
We're together.
The light is brighter.
It's a lamp; not light.
We're together
because we're afraid
while mother is flying
in an oven
like a moth.
We're afraid.
We huddle closer,
waiting for mother to burn.
When the flames die
we have no eyelashes,
never sleeping.
We're beyond self-description,
that's impossible,
like our having no choices.
We're infants
but not literally.

We are icebergs floating in the minds of infants.

1992

This Instant

The instant the street-corner cellist sounds his memories
the last patch of light in the twilight dies,
ending its life at an old railway station.

A set of grey internal organs opens in the sky.
There's nothing that goes beyond it
except a weight whirling on the river —
what used to be the mass
of the sinking of faith,
now, only stillness.

After the cello, stillness.
Trees quietly change colour.
Children in silence drink milk.
Boats shipping sand slide off.
We watch as roof tiles stoically watch.
We sniff . . . The air where
they and we stood together
has silently vanished.

Who exists? Only the light doesn't show.
Who takes leave of himself, only for a second?
Who says the moment is one's whole life?
But this instant, Scotland's pounding rain
suddenly strikes a blow against a basin —

1992

When I Knew the Bell Sound Was Green

I receive the sky from wherever the trees point.
Among the trees hide olive green characters
as light hides in lexicons.

Extinguished stars record, flocks of
blinded birds keep the balance of light
and its dark shadows, death and death to come.

Two pears dangle on a bough.
The fruit has the inkling of shadows
like the bell sound hidden in trees.

In these woods December wind resists stronger liquor.
A gust of wind, hastening speech, is
blocked, blocked by the pillars of the granary

dreamt in nightmares of marble, dreams of
a startling rustle of wind on the gravestones —
startled awake. The last leaves rush to the sky.

Autumn's writing sprouts from the death of trees.
The bell sound, at that moment, lights up my face
in skies that ship gold for the last time —

1992

Only One Is Allowed

Only one memory is allowed
to stretch as far as the steel rails reach — teach you to
measure the future with grain, pave roads with cloth.
Only one season is allowed
when wheat is sown, when the sunlight of May
from a bent back pulls the earth in all directions.
Only one hand is allowed
to make you see: there are ploughed furrows in your palm,
the land's thoughts smoothed out cleanly by the other hand.
Only one horse is allowed
to be paralyzed by a woman's gaze at five in the afternoon,
to teach your temper to put up with your flesh.
Only one person is allowed
to show you that the dead are dead, having died,
and how the wind will make you intimate with that death.
Only one type of death is allowed.
Every word is a bird with its head dashed to bits.
The sea ceaselessly overflows a smashed earthen pot.

1992

22

They

for Sylvia Plath

Naked are their dark shadows
like the breath of birds.

They're beyond this world
like oysters on the seabed

opening and closing —
leaving solitude behind.

The seclusion that could breed pearls
remains in their dark shadows.

Mementoes, out there, are icebergs,
they're mausoleums built of sharks' heads,

voyages of ships that wake the ocean grey
like London, that opened, black umbrella.

Kept in your death
are snowflakes, braille, and some figures,

but they cannot be remembrance.
Let solitude turn into beckoning.

Let the loneliest people move furniture all night.
Let them use a vacuum cleaner

to suck up all the scent you left
in the world. It is thirty years.

1993

23

For the Sake of

Dragging in a pair of red shoes, wading through beer caps,
for the sake of an everlasting hostility between them,
two swollen legs reach into water to make a stir.
For the sake of the bones bullied in the flesh,
for the sake of minnows swimming between toes,
for the sake of a type of education,
asphalt pitch flows away from dark skin.
For the sake of the earth, wounded underfoot,
for her sake, we must blaze new miles without pause.

Point with the hand that's lost its fingers.
For the sake of multitudinous nations naked in migration,
for the sake of a place without death or seasons,
for the sake of the cries, with no asking price,
for the sake of all things, not merely those possessed,
for the sake of that which cannot be obliterated,
that's been twisted, and because of this twisting
expands to a complete map —
from the bloody dust, where you dig out the headline pictures —

1993

24

Is as Before

Walking through the night when snow whirls around heads and
is as before, over a sheet of white paper that is as before,
walking into those fields that cannot be seen, and are as before.

Walking among words, in grass fields, among
discounted leather shoes, walking till the moment when words
catch sight of their homeland, and are as before.

Standing in wheat fields straightening the suit that is as before,
bending knees cast from gold shields that are as before,
this world's clearest and loudest, the clearest and loudest.

As before, as before is the great earth

When a shaft of autumn light shines through the legs of
the wheat cutter,
it's a torrent of wild laughter carried across a saffron
cornfield, it's
a scarlet plot of peppers seen in a blast of firecrackers, it is
still as before.

The golden yellow that can't be recreated through any
chemistry,
its order a surge of all-out effort at growth by the autumn earth,
its persuasive power is felt everywhere,
it is as before.

A shock of cold manure thrown to the sky by a spade is
as before,
October's rocks moving into formation are as before,
November's rain passing through a place without you any more
is as before.

As before seventy pears in a tree
laughing their faces off.
Your father is as before a fit of
coughing in the middle of your mother's laughter.

The heads of oxen bob down the disappearing road,
and as before a family
watching the snow sitting in an ox cart
is reached and licked by a huge ox tongue.

Ah, warmth is as before warmth

The warmth of memory's snow, adding to the weight of
memory.
What the snow still owes is covered at this moment by snow.
It's snow that turns over this page.

Turned over, and as before

Winter's wheat fields and graveyards stand side by side.
Four desolate trees are planted there. The past's light,
poured into retelling, bursts apart beyond speech.

Burst apart, and as before

Your father builds his sky out of your mother's death.
Making your mother's gravestone out of his death,
your father's bones walk down from the high hills.

And as before

Every star is experiencing this life in this world.
Every shard of glass buried in the backyard is speaking,
saying — for a reason that won't be seen again —

Is as before, is as before

1993

Five Years

Five glasses of strong liquor, five candles, five years.
Forty-three years of age, a surge of sweat at midnight,
fifty hands swing to slap the table top.
A flock of birds with clenched fists flies out of yesterday.

Five strings of red firecrackers burst through May,
thunder rumbles between the five fingers of a hand,
but in April four fungi freeloading
on the tongues of four dead horses don't die.
Five minutes past five on the fifth five candles go out,
but scenery that shouts at dawn doesn't die.
Hair dies but not the tongue.
Temper retrieved from well-boiled meat will not die.
Mercury seeps into semen for fifty years and neither will die.
Self-delivering fetuses don't die.
Five years have passed, five years do not die.
In five years, twenty generations of insects die out.

1994

Never Make Dreams

Separated from the living world, make pies, use
the child's tooth marks left on the bread
to make beds, grab another nipple from the bottle
to make birds who care only for flying,
not crying, not buying insurance.
Make what does not grow out of prayers,
what is not found in the present order.

1994

从不作梦

隔著人世做饼, 用
烤面包上孩子留下的齿痕
做床, 接过另一只奶嘴
作只管飞翔的鸟
不哭, 不买保险
不是祈祷出来的
不在这秩序里

1994

POEMS IN CHINA

When the People Rise Up Out of the Hard Cheese

The noise of singing eclipses
the bloody stench of revolution.
August tenses like a lethal bow.
The malevolent son, with hoarse voice
and tobacco, strides from the hut. Oxen
strive on, kept cruelly blinded. Charred corpses
hang from their haunches like festival drums.
Heaped as far as the bamboo fence, the animals
slaughtered for sacrifice gradually blur.
Far off, another army sends up clouds of smoke.

1972

Departure

The green fields stretch out like a mind at ease.
Labour is merely dusk falling and falling as
the future's legion forces swagger in.
You are someone pushed onto an unfamiliar path,
turning for that side alley, grown older.
Ten thousand village lights go out, leave
only a shepherd with his scarlet whip
just guarding the darkness, guarding the night.

1972

Night

On a night crammed with symbols
the moon is like a patient's ashen face
like a formless lapse in time
and death like a doctor stands by the bed:
a draining of the heart,
a terrible shift in the mind.
Moonlight coughs softly from the empty front yard.
Ah, moonlight insinuates so blatant an exile.

1973

Summer

Still the flowers protrude their false blooms
and the mean trees sway, ceaselessly
dropping their luckless offspring.
The sun like a martial arts master has
skipped the wall and fled, leaving
a youth confronting the downcast sunflowers.

1975

Autumn

Left fallen on the stone steps
only maple leaves, playing cards.
Left in memory
only the continual sound of rain.
That intermittent rain-sound comes round again
like a passing reminder
like a pause in a funeral oration which
then goes on.

1975

"The blood of one entire class"

The blood of one entire class is shed,
the archers of one class still loosing arrows.
China's ancient dream is haunted,
while in the banal vaulted sky
a worn-out page of moon
rises over desert.
In this pitch-dark vacant city, yet again
the urgent knocking of red terror.

1974

"Throughout this drunken land"

Throughout this drunken land
the people's coarse faces and groaning hands.
Before them, endless hardship.

Barn lanterns sway in the wind.

The night sleeps soundly
but eyes open wide. You can hear
the emperor snore through his rotten teeth.

1973

"You are a people"

You are a people both bloated and hollowed,
a body long stiffening in death.
The strokes of centuries have lashed your back
and you've borne it in silence
like a genteel western lady as she
dabs away a sigh with her handkerchief.
You've spent the night under these hanging eaves.
Ah, how the rain drips — drips.

1973

Blessing

Should society have trouble giving birth,
that scrawny, leather-skinned widow
has charms tied to a bamboo rod
she'll wave at the rising moon.
Her bloody belt emits a monstrous stench,
makes vicious dogs all over howl till dawn.

From that superstitious suitor
the motherland's led off by another father,
wandering through London parks, Michigan streets,
staring with orphan eyes at hurried steps that come and go,
again, again stammering old hopes, humiliations.

1973

Auspicious Day

As if life's books were settled,
as if sacrificial wine were drunk up,
the first light of day
breaks into prison
and the bough flaunts its blossoms.
A lifetime's shame at once redeemed —
dreams, however stale in memory,
resound like a bugle.

Wind cannot blow away the desires of youth.
On harvested land
under the brilliant sun,
those wretched, idle villages.
Logic, as usual, revives,
putting the life
of freedom out to pasture.

1973

Young Girl's Polka

The same pride, same trickery,
freedom's girls
these would-be empresses
will go for love to the sky's far corner,
follow ne'er-do-wells, never be unfaithful.

1973

Little Boy

You created man, not freedom.
You created woman, not love.
    God, how mediocre.
    God, you are so mediocre!

1973

Youth

Nothingness, from kissed lips,
slips out, bearing a stream of
unnoticed consciousness:

on that street where I madly chased women,
today white-gloved workmen
calmly spray insecticide.

1973

Dusk

Solitude awakens beneath sheets,
details silently advancing.
The poet twitches like a beetle
casting alien reflections
in a dusk sabotaged as usual
by the people's servants.

1973

Dusk

When the daring lover
with tapered buttocks
tentatively rises,
it's as if the city is tipped off,
brutely shakes off its locks
and threatens the women
who gallop into night.

1979

To the Rival

On the cross of freedom shoot the patriarch dead.
For the first time your coward's hand writes *rebel*.
When you walk again from doomsday to spring,
your spent corpse sprawls across the road of resurrection.

Cherish this passion: blood will not congeal in glory.
Burying my head on the bronze statue of a giant, I drift asleep
and dream that in the winter of truth
it's me, silently shooing crows from the graveyard sky.

1973

Poet

Bathed in moonlight
I'm hailed as a wimp-emperor,
succumbing to words like bees
swarming thick and fast, poring
over my young body. They
bore into me, ponder me, reduce me
to a do-nothing.

1973

Handicraft

for Marina Tsvetaeva

I write a poetry of degenerate youth
(unchaste poems)
in a long narrow room.
Poems ravished by poets.
Street-corner poems dismissed by cafés.
My indifferent
no longer remorseful poetry
(itself a story).
My poems unread
like the history of a story.
I've lost pride
lost love
(my aristocratic poetry).
She eventually will be taken
in marriage to a peasant.
She, is my wasted days.

1973

War

Sunlight leans against the tolerant headstone.
A deep melancholy voice narrates.
Tall thin people remove army caps.
Life lived long ago. A village of relatives.

1972

Sea

The sea retreats into nightfall,
hauling the day and sadness.
The sea is silent,
not wanting again to pardon us, or
hear our praise.

1973

At Fifteen

At fifteen I set my mind upon wisdom.
At thirty I had a foundation.
At forty I had certainty.
At fifty I knew the laws of heaven.
At sixty I was ready to listen.
At seventy I could follow my heart's desire without transgression.
                    Confucius, Analects

A fifteen-year-old scatters steel,
overripe crops start firing shots.

Earth tucks its head under a blanket,
a globe with a bump.

Struggle is a slew of mops
swabbing away where no blood flows.

A summer's belly opens,
all the foolish melons raise their heads.

The world's a snare,
the world's a babe

lifting cruel eyes:
sometimes bloodshed has a beginning,

a start is sometimes stopped.
The kid who kicks his leather shoes into a tree —

the dark tightly grasps
tips of outstretched claws —

1984

Honeyweek

First Day

Leaves fall on the path we plan to take.
In a dreamlike summer,
the surroundings familiar as friends.
As for us, we're miles apart like sheep to pasture.

You, eyes shining in daylight,
look as if you've taken medicine.
I — is this too gruff?
      "Be rougher with me
      so I'll know I'm a woman!"

Before leaving the woods,
we became lovers.

Second Day

Mountains stand before us, savage and serene —
the serenity only fat people possess.
Strangeness clashes
one bout between us.
Eyes lowered, you withdraw your hand.
And feeling somewhat sordid,
slap me on the face.
> "If only the power would go out:
> the animals in the zoo
> could break free of their prisons,
> Baiwan Village — swept away by torrential floods!"

Third Day

The sun is as full as the son.
You conceived it; we sit.
With fingers turned green
I part the grass reeds.
Flowing water flickers with gold light
like menstrual blood.
I can't help it, telling obscene tales,
heard by every prurient passer-by.

After, satisfied in the murky light,
we make up stories,
pluck the wild thorns from our trouser legs,
do it once more,
then run quick as we can
to my feeble, aged parents.

Fourth Day

You don't show up, but I
have to nod at them,
talk to them,
even laugh with them.
No, I refuse
the follies spread on bread,
those noses that sniff, eyes inspecting goods,
the grandfathers who live long, long lives.
I can't spend Sundays balancing
plates in my hands any more.
I must forget,
forget! The cabdriver's corns, the wanderer's spit.
Forget! Beards that brag unblushingly; folks without sin.

You never turn up, but I hear your voice.
"The people we drew never wore a stitch.
The trees we drew had eyes.
We saw freedom: it was a buffalo.
We saw the ideal: it was dawn.
Both of us will be written as legend,
our legs long as rifles,
our red hands able to
catch the sun without fail.
          You've learned everything from me.
          Go now. Conquer the world!"

Fifth Day

See that peeling chimney
like our skin-deep love?
From a window that's borne no joy
I watch the cripples by the riverbank chase butterflies.

When I, from selfishness,
retreat to solitude,
your teeth no longer gleam for me.
We both get real; we
really part.

Sixth Day

Is what you've said true?
True.
Since when have you thought so?
From the beginning.
You're no longer in love?
That's right; it's time to marry.
You still love me.
No. Marry.
You love yourself only.
(Distracted, I nod.)
Why didn't you tell me sooner?
I've always been deceiving you.
(The whole street notices
a guy in a duck-tongue cap
bullying a girl.)

Seventh Day

Rejoining a faith, we march into Sunday.
        Passing the factory gates,
        passing the peasants' fields,
        passing the traffic-police boxes,
confronting the banner-waving throng.
We're demonstration slogans slurred together.
We argue: who's the worst bastard in the world?
        Number one: Poet.
        Number two: Woman.
        We agree.
It's true; we're sons and daughters of bitches.
Facing the east where no sun rises,
we do morning exercises.

1972

I Remember

I remember in the night I remember:
the black-red sky
like a kiss before death.
The city gate, furtively opening,
allows the road to lead to freedom where
furry villages curl up so long in darkness,
green fungus beards grow in their shadows.
All things listen intently in silence.
Only a horsecart starts out for
the wide-eyed brightness.
    But rain trickles dark speculations.
Someone interrogates sand and stone,
accuses a woman's feet hidden beneath skirts
and moving among flowers,
the ox that carries a child to the sea,
a morning with smoke rising over a deer field,
even the lake at dusk where swans sleep.
    Timid houses are first to tremble.
Fire on the outskirts lets loose its rampage:
crops are lit, trees maddened,
a land of flowers is levelled with corpses,
the river halts its bullied squirming,
the mountains, also, surrender glory

and when — when

doors broke free of shackles, ladders walked alone,
bricks and tiles quit roofs, trees strode off
swearing by those flattened roads, rounded mountains,
bold, commonplace, modest smoke.

Even our guns never fired!

Walls leaned, but would not collapse.
Chimneys stood with traces of charring.
Books lay open. Never shut again.
Fruit clung to branches, green and hard.

Time had only night, never to have dawn,
only faces poking in windows and
menace from regulations.

Ah, smashed, smashed, be smashed at last.

The road has met its dead end. The pit's
full at last, grain
stored deeper and deeper underground.
The past too like a granite statue
watches the grey house fall.

1976

The Climb to the View

Having surpassed these sickening heights, the evening
sunlight, clustered in the buildings high above,
once more polishes the bronze arms of dusk, and overlooks
the lanterns jostling in the human festival.
The parade glints against red roof tiles,
makes memory's trumpeter dazed and faint, while
ten millennia squat, ready to pounce, right there.

Having braved the dazzling red ocean storm
to the path's end, the splendour
now carries away its labour.
Under the pressure of boundless treasures
the great lantern shade catches fire, is consumed
in the twilight's greater shade.
The tiredness at day's end —
bit by bit, one toll after another,
the bells spread their long hair over the still fields.

1983

Silkworm: Textile

Bogged down deep in its paper city —
this space the size of a knuckle —
its more and more transparent head
accumulates the radiance of millennia
as it spits out silk.
A humble skill embroiders
the umbrella in which
to bury itself.
Its end of motion
lies in this motion,
pinned down by "tranquillity,"
spitting out the course of its life
with its song in its mouth.
The fruit of meditation
caves in its emptied head —
a single thread "the instant"
binding the ages.

1983

Gallery

A

Mist gallops from the platform, blindly on.
Dawn brightens.
Dirt roads merge into the skyline's clean edge,
the black untilled fields turn back towards evening.

B

That barelegged, lovesick fool
with his sharp beak
fretfully pecks at twigs, scatters the sky
while gun, powder, and hunter
shut the net of dusk.

C

Robed in dew, standing in the dawn
she watches over the vineyard
like an upper-class lady
viewing her shrubs and flowers
with ruined beauty, with winsome sorrow,
she is smiling on them.

D

Awake with ease and verve as if the host,
before your eyes
walls ablaze with the setting sun.
Wrapped in a striped towel, raising a white arm
it is you, combing —

E

With that beautiful throat she sings to the night sky,
gathers in a basket those stars her notes shake down.
She walks into the depths of the wood
singing to the myths.

F

Look, a windowful of glorious sunlight
shines on my palette, my rifle,
my bachelor's cot,
and you, during the days of waiting,
        you've come.

G

Darkness set to descend,
your spurning voice
strains with emotion.
Your hair snags the twilight
over those deepening eyes
where no lamplight is visible.

H

Ah well
not only does night
conceal your face
it transforms your
voice as well.
So I feel
our missing each other
slipping forward
like a sleigh
gliding over our wounds.

1973–79

Wishful Thinking Is the Master of Reality

And we are birds beak-to-beak
in time's affair
from people
drawing lines in the sand.

The key twists once in the ear.
Shadows break away from us.
The key wrenches on and on.
We've degenerated into people,
unrecognizable people.

1982

Looking Out from Death

Looking out from death you'll always see
the people all your life you'd never see.
You find a burial site easily enough.
Just sniff around, then bury yourself there
in a spot they begrudge you.

They shovel dirt in your face.
You should thank them. And thank them again.
For your eyes will never again see your enemies.
Then into your death come
their shouts as they're consumed by hate,
but you no longer listen.
Now those are the cries of outright anguish!

1983

Dead, Ten Dead

Another ten. Ten
more lions.

Matters after death: no more
but no less — exactly

ten stiffened tongues
are left. Much like five pairs

of warped wooden slippers,
the already rusty

ten tails, like
ten vet's assistants' hands

with ten ropes
slackening. Opening

twenty hazy eyelids:
sitting in a bathtub

ten lions, dumb
but alive. But dead —

they're ten lions
who starved a story

to death. Stories
come from ten

meddlesome story-
telling throats.

1983

Fear

Oh, I fear, I fear
what? I ask you —
do you fear?
I'm asking me.

Judgement is a fearful
enemy.

I have no enemies, and I
fear all the more. If night
were a huge piece of orange peel
and the flesh were between my lips,
I fear — this is possible.

This is possible. Do you fear?
My face is transparent, you are in it
watching me. We're staring at each other,
flesh sprouting rapidly from the same face.

Unless blinded we'll always be
looking — at each other
in a glass of pitch black
milk. Unless blind. Blind

I fear even more. Being,
by a simple nurse, stitched,
in surgery
for the transplant of eyes,
under a sheet the heads of
two children are revealed.

One cries out,
or they holler together;
I fear both. I fear the thought:

extracting myself from the shattered
window, I have only
a head of glass shards sticking out
and two abhorrent hands
trapped in the coffin's lid —
those are yours. I don't
want to think about it.

From the top half of a tree
saw off my bottom half,
and you're in pain,
screaming. You yell,
I don't fear. No pain.
There is, in fact, no pain.
I follow suit shouting,
That's right; you no longer fear.

1983

Window Fond of Weeping

Speaking beneath the farthest cloud,
sliding along the forehead
of the light's ceramic tiles

lying idle outside the seasons.
Idle, silence is a mirror
reflecting me, forgetfulness

a branch of fat pears
hanging, quivering.
"Come on, we're yours," they say.

Early spring tears a slit
in the seasons. "We've
returned, it's for you, all along

the whole lot was yours," they
chatter, and spit out from the treetop
four sweet pits.

Across the basin the sun swimming,
schools of fish in the flowing water
dashing against my head.

1983

Smoking Gun of Daybreak

Thin smoke curls up from the barrel of dawn.
Stove fire's setting rays, one night's music, everything
                                                    dreaming.

I brush the cobblestones with brittle claws,
the night rat like a child also

rustles a land of silver with walking.
Ah, everything locked in dream.

Though dawn shines down and lights the past's mirror,
everything has aged.

The doors and windows of home glow with an orchard's reds.

Everything has aged,
though passion's wheels spin nonstop.

Listen, I've snapped off the tiny horns
all over the night rats' bodies.

Listen to the proud songs of the
night rats upright on top of the train.

Somewhere, where there is only happiness,
there, happiness is like timber.

Happiness is timber,
crackling.

The doors and windows of home glow with an orchard's reds.

1983

One Story Tells His Entire Past

When he opens his body's windows facing the sea
and leaps toward the clinking of innumerable knives,
one story tells his entire past.
When all tongues extend toward that sound,
retrieving the thousand clashing knives,
all days will squeeze into one single day.
So, every year will have an extra day.

Last year topples over under the great oak.
His memory is of a cow pen, overhead
a column of smoke.
Some children on fire hold hands
and sing around the kitchen knife.
Before the flames die down,
they rage in the trees.
The flames finally singe his lungs.

His eyes are the festival days of two hostile towns,
his nose two tobacco pipes squinting at the sky.
Women fire love wildly at his face,
forcing his lips agape. Soon a train
on a head-on crash course with death will pass,
leaving him with a space of morning
between his outstretched arms,
the dawn pressing down the sun's head.

A silenced revolver tolls morning's arrival,
one more cheerless than a box tossed face down.
A burst of snapping branches is the broken
clapper on an old log door
cast in the funereal street.
One story tells his entire past.
Death is only a superfluous heartbeat.

While stars dive at the venom-soaked earth,
time rots beyond the ticking of clocks.
Rats grind their milk teeth on the coffin's rusted copper,

fungus stamps feet on decayed lichen,
the cricket's son plies endless needlework on his body,
and there's evil, tearing away his drum-skin face.
His body now is permeated
with the story that tells his past.
Bodily, one story tells his past.

All his past reflects the story:
a lanky man lolls on a tree stump.
The sun for the first time
reads his eyes closely,
and closer till it sits on his knee.
The sun emits smoke between his fingers.
Each night I train my telescope on the spot
until the sun dies out:
a tree stump rests where he sat.

Quieter than a plot of cabbage in May,
his horsecart drives by in the small hours.
Death shatters into a heap of pure glass.
The sun rumbles down the road where mourners return.
Children's feet glide onto evergreen olive branches.
My head pounds as if countless horse hooves drummed.
Compared to a big, crude knife,
death is a mere grain of sand.
So, one story tells his entire past.
So, a thousand years turn round to look. Look —

1983

Milestones

The first-glimpsed heading of that seductive highway
makes you dizzy.
That's your starting place. Clouds wrap your head,
intending to offer you a job.
That's your starting point.
When a jailhouse slams its metal onto a city,
cobblestones hug you close in the centre of the street.
Each winter's snowfall is your threadbare coat,
but the sky beyond is a blue university.

The sky, the deathly pale sky,
with its cheeks just pinched
makes you laugh, your beard bobs like eating.
When you follow the tall tree slicing through time,
golden rats wade across water dreaming of you.
You're a curled broad bean in hurling winds.
You're a chair, belonging to the ocean,
which wants you to learn, again, from the beginning
on the seacoast of human cities.
To seek yourself on the route to yourself.
Heavy northern snow is your road,
the flesh on your shoulders is your food.
You, a traveller never glancing back,
nothing you despise will ever vanish.

1985

Skies of Winter Nights

My bed's feet are four white rats.
I float onto the night skies like a basket
and skate out over the heavens.

So clear, undulant,
the skies of winter nights.
More vacant than an abandoned scrapyard.

Snowflakes are drunken moths
and the villages fitfully dotted
are wine barrels drifted in snow.

"Who will clasp me around the neck!"
I hear a horse
murmur as it trots.

"Clip, clip." Giant shears go to work.
From within a great cave, the stars all rise,
and waves billow in the horse's eyes.

Ah, I feel so good
like sliding down the glistening spine of a whale.
I'm searching for the city where I live.

I'm searching for my love.
Here on my bike's pedals, these two lusty bananas.
Let the wood

rest in the lumberyard and get on with its nightmare.
Let the new moon lie on the ashen Gobi desert,
go on and sharpen its sickle.

Not necessarily from the east,
I see the sun as a necklace of pearls.
The sun is a string of pearls, rising in succession.

1985

Walking

For the same reason you're late
you go forward.
Now embarking,
setting out,
you will never arrive.
You know that you know
but you go on
in an overturned box
with head to the ground,
tramp along the box's lid,
walk till you get to where
your foot stamps on your hand.

You walk through this city in the stupidest way.

1985

Characters

They're their own masters
till they crawl to each other,
countering their intents.
As you read them, they spar.
Every morning I'm irritated by the stuff.
I hate what's been printed,
it's simply been written by him.

The dreams I had once
were the gasses that leaked from his brain.
The composure after one's last
good tooth is pulled out
trembles on his face.
Ghostly as a patient
who forgot his blood transfusion,
he flees the ward.
He has long since despised himself.

1986

from Winter Night Woman

A

Besides breath left on the window by passing stars,
no animals, none whatsoever, are here to torture me.

Mosquitoes are trapped in glass tubes.
I see their scarlet snouts

and I care about their fate, too.
The snow keeps up its pressure through four seasons.

One full year, the snow has pink flesh,
its eyes everywhere.

Thick snow falls nonstop,
but there's not, not the least hint

of anyone's being missed.
I belong to myself — this thought

keeps watch over me.
I so simply sink

my nails into my flesh.
Each night like this for a hundred years.

B

Buses bear snow on their roofs.
Pedestrians are all strangers
with windows on the backs of their shadows.

Two windows have spotted me
and a third, also.
I think

what do I need? With my hands
I gesture to myself
this idea — no

it's not the one
who will come
after today

nor is it
the second time seeing
someone seen twice.

I'm moving forward to deeper
fathom myself. I'm torturing
what is absent in others.

E

Leaves fall like lead.
Winter skates on long toes.
Bulky machines are screwed to the ground

and the roots of trees —
all of them fixed with wheels.
How sympathetic I am

with these made things: characters
roll in hands, insects
gnaw at glass, books

are hungry babies, a grape
in the lung — maybe it's a kelp frond
made of glass.

Matters on the mind turn like stomachs,
heaps of black clouds roll
over and over on the bed.

I plunge my hands into sleep,
quilts keep
churning in the sky.

F

The night ages, boots scattered about the room.
I fall asleep; the table lamp catches fire.
Day breaks and the sun, like a fan, flares up.
Half-year-old leaves begin to snow.

Lovely time is eaten up by wildflowers.
Life is the grass the horses devour.
Impossible to believe: the fields are illusions.
Impossible to believe: the real is a lie.

The sea, perhaps, is a shoe once full of sand.
The dried fish, with its gaping mouth, might be a boat
from three thousand years back . . . Is your life
on the right track? You — are you pleased with yourself?

The fish is fried, the dish changes shape,
the feathers on man turn more evil.
My eyes are sated with
everything in the heartbreaking shop.

Get me a new pair of hands. The true meaning of
poet: to persist in the madness
of arranging the stripes
        on the tiger's back.

1985

Dance Partner

A timid little animal
whispers from your throat.
A fine sensation:
your fingertips
drawn over my back.
Ah, attention to them
leaves my senses obsolete.

Your small depressed figure
reminds me of a boy.
You two eyeing each other
and I suddenly old.

1985

It's

It's   a fine piece of cloth
wrecked by dawn on the horizon.
It's the moment   night and day
claim each other.
It's first light   behind the ravaged metal wall
revealing a   disfigured face.
> *I love you.*
> *I'll never take it back.*

It's   a leaning stove
the sun collapsing on the mountain ridge.
Loneliness racing for the abyss.
It's the wind
a blind postman   delivering down to the earth's core.
Earth's green blood
erases all sound.   I believe
the words it takes away:
> *I love you.*
> *I'll never take it back.*

It's an old song   a string of bells
staring their eyes out.
It's the river water's shackles
beating small drums.
It's the twin suns of your blue eyes
descending   out of the blue.
> *I love you.*
> *I'll never take it back.*

It's two hammers   striking in turn
the flames from the same dream.
It's the moon   heavy as a bullet
making the boat we once took   go down.
It's mascara   stuck on eternally.
> *I love you.*
> *I'll never take it back.*

It's all that's lost
swelling into a river.
It's flames   the flames are another river.
It's the flames' shape   constant hooks
their claws all sticking up
splintering   on star-shaped
outstretched   still-burning fingers.   It's —
        I love you,
        I'll never take it back.

1985

Desire

Sitting in a corner of the city
sitting there
sitting on your left foot
on your little toe
on the tip of the tiniest toenail
                    gliding
on glass kneecaps. I
am the crystal's liquid, the alcoholic air of nothingness,
the blue skeleton emerging in the transparent fat.
I am at three in the morning the twitching chair's
                                        leg.
I approach you with hallucination
and measure you by defects.
With my withered hand, that five-
petalled rose, all anaesthetized,
with my eyes, the entrance of
a square wound: ignorance sucks me in.
Two ropes tie each other up,
two keys spin in each other's locks,
two clocks absorb each other's time.
And then your
thirty-two glistening teeth, ah —
a greater ignorance sucks me further in.
Desire has drunk what is most intense,
sickening is more exciting than making well.
                                    "But
don't stand in the desert rubbing your hands!"
Your voice drifts down over eons,
your eyelashes are sleeping wild grasses,
your black eyebrows shine like scissors
stretching to the hyacinth bean twigs,
your fingers are teenagers embracing,
you're a violin donning a red silk scarf.
        "You mustn't worry!"
You're a nurse, quietly attending the sea,

you're my lover, your breath
is weak but prolonged.
At the moment the birds' pink claws
shake hands,
that second,
one shadow enters another,
you are a myriad of mirrors reflected in one.
Maybe it's you and me, maybe it's
me and someone, maybe
it's the two youngest dancers
                    determined
    to sustain this world with their toes!

1986

30 June 1986

Across the Pacific Ocean
my lover sends a message from America:

"That stretch of wheat is dead — the one
with the burial ground in the middle."

This is a manoeuvre — the equivalent of
another good kick in the ass.

Even with postage
it comes to only 44 U.S. cents.

Beneath the image is
foreshadowing. For instance,

across a Manhattan shoe shop
a streamer reads:

"We hail from different stars."
Or inscribed on a birthday cake

of three skin colours
shipped to Cincinnati from Philadelphia:

"Heal the distance between us
with a child."

There's no scene under this one,
only the one set in San Francisco:

fished out of his back pocket
is an ancient piece of Oriental lard soap.

A sailor escorting a blind man across the street
hurls it into the booming cosmos.

1988

Bell Sound

No bell sounds to waken memory
but today I heard it strike
nine times, no idea
how many more.
I heard it coming from the stables,
walked a mile
and heard again:
>   "When in the struggle for better conditions
>   will you deepen your servility?"

Then I envied the horses left in the stables.
Then, my rider struck my face.

1988

My Uncle

When I from high on the latrine pit of childhood
look down,
my uncle and a bull
exchange glances.
In their shared gaze
I think there is an objective:
to allow all light rays in the shadows no hiding place.

When a hovering soccer field floats over the school,
a hint of possibly dissolving reality
widens my uncle's eyes.
He can directly see the sun
frozen in the empty sky at the North Pole
and my uncle wants to use tweezers — to splice
the sun back in history.

Because of this I believed the sky was moveable.
My uncle often returned from there
striding as an architect
down the steps of his own design.
I believed even more: my uncle wanted
with the creak of an opening door
to shut himself in — by travelling backwards in time

my uncle wanted to repair clocks,
as if he'd inhaled enough
premonitions in the past.
That error he wished to correct
has persevered through missed time:
we've all due to this been reduced
to the liberated.

Even now that fraught cloud of tobacco smoke
chokes me.
Along the disappearing streetcar lines
I see a wheat field with
my uncle's beard sprouting up,
my uncle already wearing his red tie
runs straight out of the Earth —

1988

The Road to My Father

The chair back bent from twelve seasons of sitting
slams my swollen hands, and struts the grass fields.
Winter's scrawl sprouts from the devastation.

Someone in the sky shouts, "Buy up all the shadows
cast by clouds over the furrowed fields!"
A stern voice, my mother's

mother's, walks out of her will
dressed in thick snow like a coat thrown on
and buries the hut in such weather.

Inside the cabin, here is that famous pasture:
A boy, his golden eyelashes grown inward, kneels
and digs up my beloved: "You're not to die any more!"

I kneel behind the boy
and dig up my mother: "It's not that I cannot love again!"
My ancestors kneel behind me. They

and the straight young saplings that will go to make chairs
rise into the cold and heartless atmosphere,
uprooting weeds. Behind us

kneels the sullen planet.
We, in iron shoes, seek out signs of new life
then go on digging up — the road to my father.

1988

September

Blind men advance touching waves of wheat.
Buckwheat
gives off a fabled fragrance —
the sky of twenty years ago

glides past the profile of a boy reading.
I gaze out the window at trees standing still,
reciting from memory:
In the forest is a clearing.

Crumbled bits of petals scatter
onto the host's face finding
an eternal resting place.
A gust of old wind obliges me to bow.

September clouds shift to compost heaps.
The darkening before the storm
airbrushes the sky
covered with its towel for wiping tears.

Mother bending low cuts hay,
garment workers lean over their cloth.
The books I once read as evening approached
turn again into the black heavy earth.

1988

Northern Sea

Giant glass shards surging,
a loneliness, the solitude
before sea creatures

found land. Earth,
could you know what
removing the sky implies?

The night tigers are shipped overseas
one tiger's shadow crosses my face.
Oh, I admit to my life —

but it's a bore. My life
lacks the thrill of
humans swapping blood.

If I can't seize a memory
more potent than the wind,
I'll say:

This sea is getting old.
If I can't trust my hearing,
the locus where sounds die,

if I can't study laughter,
the sound that awaits return from the sea,
I'll say:

By things on a scale
as negligible as my body
I cannot be excited.

But what's beyond the sky attracts my attention:
rocks lay eggs, the real world's shadows shift,
on a seabed flipped upright the sea races day and night.

Ah, for the first time I know happiness.
These are things I've never seen:
silken river surfaces, rivers as bridges,

the arc of a river rolling through sky.
All nature moves me,
a singular joy does odd things to my mind.

At this instant having no more time than usual,
I hear clams
in a moment of mutual love

opening their double shells.
At the second the sentimental shed tears,
I notice

the wind ripping up the four corners of the earth,
land pervaded by the silence
after wolves have devoured the last child.

But from a giant basket rising high
I see everyone who ever loved me held
tightly, tightly — in one embrace.

1984

Northern Voices

Size and might in unison, it expands its lungs,
stretches its paws, bends backward, rolls on its chest.
Its breath spurs on the little warmth of winter
but it prefers relentless cold —

I grew up in the storm.
The storm held me close but let me breathe
so that it seemed a child wept within me,
and I wished to understand those tears
as if hoeing myself with a harrow.
Each grain of sand opened its mouth.
Mother's law wouldn't let the rivers weep.
   But I recognize this cry
   can overrule authority.

Some voices, maybe every one,
can be abused and buried in the sands.
We move around above their heads, underground
they catch their rugged breath.
Without feet or footsteps, the earth
starts stalking with thunderous tread.
   And words by a wordless voice
   are crushed.

1985

Northern Nights

The bats' noiseless shrills quiver the drum-skin of dusk.
The setting sun, regal as a tiger turning a millstone,
air, the air returned to us through the nostrils of horses,
light, the light that pierced the keyhole's eye.
       Each vanishes like an arrow.
       Every twilight has fled like this.

What the night contains is too much, what flows away
with the river is too little. What can never be still
is colliding. Colliding
some nights begin but never end,
some rivers glisten and never reveal their colours.
Some moments struggle vehement against the dark
and some can only occur in darkness.
       That night a woman stumbles on a small animal,
       language begins but life departs.

Snow has claimed the entire afternoon watched through
                      a window.
Endless afternoon.
A clutch of fat women sits in the sky taking a break,
all they remember is taking a break.
The view is obscured by large leaves.
Outside, daytime to its heart's content
displays its idiocy.
       Picture a boat wrecked in a whale's belly,
       the heart desolate as hail flying into the beehives.

Where pasture ends and city begins,
the crops are too weary to grow, the grapes wizened.
The stars have all gone cold, like sacks of stone.
Moonlight infiltrates the room through riddled walls.
We know, and so we should,
that time is turning homeward and life is a child
singing, leaving school.
       The world's a big window, outside are horses
       neighing after eating a thousand lamps.

Footprints march across the fields and climb the hillock.
Prehistoric man raises a fossil high to strike our heads.
In our minds illumined like lamps
there's still a tract of primal forest
where deer are bleeding, gliding to the sky
on paths of snow. A bar of music
trembles, trees continue to lay down their lives.
>A beginning. What has not begun, begins.
>A reunion. Let's meet at the time for meeting again.

1985

Northern Earth

Always taking my pulse, watching the river fly off,
always leaning on a wooden table, longing for heavy snow,
the whack of an axe splits locusts out of firewood.
Always touching the wintered frozen soil, my feet
know for certain, I belong here.
I record, I survey, I feed
instruments raw meat, I know for certain: here, right here,
        always here —

In a country where a stone king
stands tall with his back to the sun,
in a big threshing ground,
in an empty classroom during vacation,
before the snow sets out from the depths of the sky,
fifty bad clouds roll over the heads of cotton-pickers,
a hundred old women soar into outer space,
a thousand boys piss over the horizon,
a hundred million stars remain bleak,
        one century —

Gloomy ancestral faces darken rows of statues,
stones set between them.
In the birch forest hang black woollen coats,
to the heads of wheat are tied
the red scarves of women reapers.
        Seasons, seasons
with discipline that will never vanish
plant us on the road that history takes —

Always in this superfluous season
winter reading goes slowly, the fields' pages
no longer turn, every reader's head
is caught in secrecy — excited by gossip.

Your desolation lies in the holes cut in you,
your memory has been dug away,
your breadth through a lack of tears
dries up, you are sorrow itself —

wherever you are, there is sorrow.
On the foreheads of those failed wheat fields
seventy *mu* of cornfields destroy your brain.
Wider vegetable plots are soundless.
What is feebler than grass you can no longer hear.
What you want to say to yourself pours out:
        "This is your gospel."

1988

"那是你们的福音…"

BENEATH THE SLEEP OF IDEOLOGY:
A CRITICAL AFTERWORD

During the International PEN Congress that was held in Toronto in the fall of 1989, I attended a public forum entitled *Private Conscience and State Security* whose speakers included Harold Pinter, Chinua Achebe, and a quiet, diminutive man from the People's Republic of China who went by the pen name DuoDuo. DuoDuo's story had a truth-is-stranger-than-fiction drama to it: on the morning of June 4 of that year he'd been present in Tiananmen Square dodging soldiers' bullets as colleagues and friends fell wounded or dead around him; that evening, he'd boarded a plane for England to start a reading tour — his first trip out of China — that had been arranged months before. His departure had been a matter of purest chance; a few days, a few hours later and the doors might already have been closed. And now here he was, less than four months later, bearing first-hand witness to events that most of us had experienced at the safe distance of the news.

I felt a curious sort of envy for this man: he was someone who had stood at the centre of history, who made the projects of writers living in comfortable, peaceful countries seem like mere amusements, inessential and small. Yet what struck me most about him as he spoke, this demure, handsome man with his casual clothes and his greying hair, was exactly his humanness, his apparent ordinariness. He showed some of the usual discomfort of writers in forums such as this that required more the activist's single-mindedness than the writer's ambiguities; and he seemed less someone who had aspired to politics than someone who had had politics thrust upon him, fate having made him a spokesperson for events whose magnitude had left him not so much emboldened as humbled. On the subject of the panel's theme, the importance of individual conscience against oppression exercised in the name of state security, his message was sobering: in a China where many writers had been imprisoned or killed and where many others were now being forced to praise the very armies that had opposed them, the only possible course for those who wished to hold onto their conscience was silence.

"They have only this left," he said.

A year or so later, along with Lee Robinson and a small contingent from PEN's Canadian Centre, on whose board I now sat, I got the chance to meet DuoDuo, over supper at a restaurant in Toronto's Chinatown. DuoDuo had spent the intervening year teaching Chinese literature at the University of London, and had returned to Canada to take up a post as writer-in-residence at Glendon College, a position arranged in part by Canadian PEN. I had imagined this meeting between DuoDuo and PEN as a kind of semi-official briefing or information session. But it actually had a much simpler motive: DuoDuo was lonely. Stuck in the barrens of North York in a job that, because of his difficulty with English, was more honorary than real, he had little contact with the outside world or with the country that had offered to host him. The romance I'd imagined in political exile came down to this: to be alone in a foreign country whose language you barely spoke and whose customs you barely understood. Here he was, finally, in a place where he was allowed to say whatever he wished, and he had no one to say it to. I was reminded of something Chinua Achebe had said at the panel where I'd first seen DuoDuo a year before: often freedom didn't end your problems, it merely began them.

Thus started my friendship with DuoDuo. In the years since then, I have had a chance to view more closely that first tension I sensed in him between the personal and the political; but if anything, the matter only grows more complex, more obscure, the more one tries to resolve it. DuoDuo is always quick to insist that he is above all a writer, that what matters is the writing, and he stubbornly resists being reduced to a political symbol; and yet there is no way around the fact that even at the simplest level politics continue to inform his relationship to the world. For a while, for instance, after DuoDuo had made the decision to try to settle in Canada, he was unable to leave the country. It was not that he was being held here against his will, or that there was any shortage of invitations from abroad, to seminars, to poetry festivals, to conferences; the simple fact was that he'd run out of pages in his Chinese passport for other countries to issue visas on. The solution, he was told, was to have the Chinese embassy here insert more pages; but the chances were pretty slim that once he'd turned the passport in he would ever get it back. The situation seemed like some joke out of Kafka, this bureaucratic insistence on form despite the obvious precariousness of DuoDuo's circumstances. The problem was only resolved after DuoDuo was granted landed immigrant status in Canada (he had chosen immigrant over refugee status to leave more open the possibility of a future return to China) and he was able to apply for a Canadian travel document to replace his used-up Chinese passport.

The tension between the personal and the political is also one that goes to the heart of DuoDuo's writing. DuoDuo is first and foremost an experiential writer, one who draws his details from the familiar, the human, the everyday; yet in a situation such as his where experience is so intricately linked with the upheavals of history, the everyday can take on apocalyptic proportions. Even in poems that have no obvious political element there is always beneath the surface a pointing to the larger picture, an intricate working out, on the level of language and image, of the complexities and contradictions that underlie what during his lifetime has always been a heavily politicized culture. At the same time, DuoDuo's project is a profoundly aesthetic one: in a society where language has been so manipulated in the service of political power, it has been the task of writers such as DuoDuo to create a poetic space outside the bounds of that manipulation, to make the case for poetry as poetry rather than as ideology. It is in this context, where the division of personal from political becomes impossible and where coining a metaphor is a political act, that DuoDuo's work needs to be understood.

DuoDuo was born Li Shizheng in Beijing in 1951, to intellectual-class parents who had both studied abroad in the 1940s. In the normal course of things he would have been reasonably assured of a comfortable future: his parents, in a climate that was officially suspicious of intellectuals but in practice needed their skills, both held respectable positions, his mother on the staff of the Chinese Literary Federation and his father as a research fellow at the Institute for World Economics in the Chinese Academy of Social Sciences; and DuoDuo had the benefit of a fairly cultured upbringing, one that allowed him to develop an interest in painting and to read widely in both Chinese and non-Chinese literature.

Then in 1966, when DuoDuo was fifteen, the Cultural Revolution was launched, Mao's great call to the country's youth to help him return socialism to its roots and purge the Party bureaucracy of backsliders and "capitalist roaders." Schools across China were closed; students organized into units they called the Red Guards and began to travel the country in a campaign that became known as the

Red Terror, ransacking libraries and museums and private homes to eliminate any remnants of pre-revolutionary culture and targeting people of suspicious class backgrounds for public humiliations. The issue of DuoDuo's own class background suddenly came to the fore: his parents were "struggled against," as the saying went, and were eventually sent to cadre schools for re-education; and DuoDuo, though like most of his peers a fervent follower of Mao at that point, was prohibited from joining the Red Guards. Then part-way into the campaign, Mao, seeing that local Party officials were using the class-line attacks of the Red Guards as a way of deflecting criticism from themselves, suddenly denounced these attacks as counter-revolutionary. Almost at once, those who had been barred from the original Red Guards began to form Rebel Red Guard units, and soon pitched battles were being fought in the street between the two factions, each side believing it was the true defender of Mao's revolution. DuoDuo was quick to join one of these rebel units, though to his own disappointment he remained more or less on the sidelines in the ensuing melée.

Eventually the turmoil spread to every corner of the country, bringing it to the brink of civil war. Mao was forced to call in the army, and when the dust had settled there was no way of telling, what with the various contradictions and reversals in official policy that had marked the campaign, who had been victorious or who had been in the right. Then when the students began to filter back to their schools in the fall of 1968, they found there was no place for them. Many were deemed to have graduated, though without the possibility of advancing to the next level; and with the object of defusing the threat posed by these returning legions of unemployed, disaffected youths, the government began a massive program of rustification, sending the youths down to the countryside to work under the guise of furthering their socialist education. Over the next few years anywhere from 15 to 25 million young people were compelled to leave the cities for rural collectives, many of them living in near–prison camp conditions among peasants who neither appreciated nor understood them.

In 1969, as part of this rustification program, DuoDuo was posted to an agricultural brigade in Anxin district, Hebei province, on the shores of Baiyangdian Lake. The years he spent there coincided with a period of increasingly hard-line cultural policy under the infamous

Gang of Four, the leadership clique headed by Mao's wife, Jiang Qing, that had slowly been gaining ascendancy since the start of the Cultural Revolution and under whom all but the most rigorously party-line works were forbidden or expunged. But it was here that DuoDuo first began writing poetry, distributing his work through handwritten copies among a small, clandestine group of writers at his posting. DuoDuo himself left the posting in the early 1970s to receive treatment in Beijing for hepatitis; once gone, he never returned, choosing instead to remain in Beijing illegally. For several years he was unemployed, due partly to his illegal status and partly to his lack of formal education. (Among the jobs he applied for but was rejected from was one tending rowboats at Behai Park and another feeding tigers at the Beijing Zoo.) It was not until after Mao's death and the subsequent fall of the Gang of Four in 1976 that he was able to gain any meaningful employment, mainly through family connections, first as a librarian at the Institute for World Economics in Beijing and then as a journalist for the Beijing-based *Peasants' Daily*.

Mao's death and the fall of the Gang of Four also opened the way for what became known as the Beijing Spring, a period of relative openness during which a newly rehabilitated Deng Xiaoping, on the outs during the reign of the Gang of Four, began to encourage criticism of the Cultural Revolution as a way of distancing himself from its excesses and solidifying his own power. It was during this period that the Democracy Wall movement sprang up, a grassroots protest that saw a flurry of political posters go up on the Xidan Wall in Beijing criticizing past repressions and calling for democratic reforms. At the same time there was a sudden flourishing of literary activity, with the establishment of dozens of unofficial journals patched together in back rooms with borrowed typewriters and pirated mimeograph machines. One such journal was the avant-garde literary magazine *Today*, founded in 1978 by a group whose nucleus went back to the small circle of writers that DuoDuo had been part of at Baiyangdian Lake.

The Beijing Spring was shortlived. By 1979, when the protests had spread to other regions of the country — spurred in part by millions of youths still stationed in the countryside who illegally began returning to the cities — the government started clamping down, accusing the protesters of promoting bourgeois freedoms and individualism and arresting some of the movement's leaders. *Today* magazine, however, was not suppressed until 1980, by which time a fledgling poetry movement had managed to take shape in its pages that included such writers as Bei Dao, Shu Ting, Gu Cheng, Mang Ke, and DuoDuo. Characterized by work that refused to yield itself to easy political analysis, the movement sparked a debate that spilled over into the country's official journals and that continued long past the closing down of *Today*. Critics of the school had from the outset accused its members of producing work that was too misty, too obscure, too lacking in any clear social purpose; and the poets themselves had turned accusation into a badge, dubbing their work "misty" poetry, *menglong shi*.

A manifesto published by the Misty poets in *Today* before the magazine's suppression asserted their right to produce work that was "no longer hack literature, no longer the mouth-piece of politics." At the simplest level the poets were reacting against the pieties and propaganda of the Cultural Revolution, when artistic work had had to conform to rigid formulas and often amounted to little more than sloganeering. But at a deeper level the poets were attempting to fight what they saw as the manipulation of even the language of dissent by the political powers-that-were, a pattern that went as far back as the Hundred Flowers Campaign of the 1950s, when Mao had briefly encouraged open criticism of Communist policy only to punish those who then spoke out, and that carried on through the Cultural Revolution and into the Beijing Spring. After the fall of the Gang of Four, for instance, the leadership had encouraged a genre of writing known as "scar" literature that had focussed on the human costs of the Cultural Revolution; but as soon as writers had begun to move away from the past into a criticism of contemporary reality they had been suppressed. The Misty poets hoped to develop a form of writing that could exist outside that sort of manipulation, that even as dissent could not be pinned down to simple meanings or be used in the service of political agendas. They were also arguing against a long-standing tradition in Chinese literature that had seen the writer as a sort of adjunct of the state, both as educator and as guardian of the public interest, a tradition that had made it easier for communism to impose on writers its own theories of social utility and systems of state control.

In any case, one practical offshoot of the complexity of Misty poetry was that it managed to elude for some time the shifting but fairly rudimentary categories of official acceptability by which writers were either praised or condemned. Thus despite the suspicion that hung over them, several of the Misty poets, including DuoDuo, were able to get their work published in official journals during the early 1980s and managed to achieve a certain level of public recognition. Then in 1983, the government launched its Anti-Spiritual-Pollution campaign to combat "decadent influences from the West." The Misties, who were often accused by their critics of Western borrowings, were specifically targeted in this campaign. One of their defenders, Xu Jingya, was forced to publish a self-criticism for having earlier argued in support of the modernist features of Misty poetry, while DuoDuo was notified by his newspaper that he was an "element under internal supervision" by the country's security forces, and was led to understand that he could expect no increase in his salary and no advancement in his career.

By 1985, however, the controls had begun to loosen again. In the ensuing period the literary importance of the Misty movement gained a measure of acceptance from the official culture, and some of the poets who had come out of it — most notably Bei Dao — became both national and international celebrities. DuoDuo, though he never had any direct relationship with official publishers and was never admitted into the Writers' Union, was able to publish two collections of poetry during this period, one officially and one unofficially, as well as a number of short stories and essays. In 1987 he was awarded the Poetry Prize at the Literature Festival of Beijing University; and in 1988, while another democracy movement was taking shape, some of those who had been associated with *Today* magazine during its brief existence came together again to present DuoDuo with the first *Today* poetry prize.

Among his peers, DuoDuo was always known as the "last bus" because his fame was so much longer in coming than for some of his fellow poets. Always considered more a poet's poet than a popular one, the complexities of his work lent themselves even less than those of his contemporaries to single-line slogans or rallying cries. In terms of the official culture he remained always an outsider, associated less with the public movement that began with *Today* than with the little acknowledged but tenacious tradition of underground writing that went back to poets such as Guo Lusheng and Zhang Langlang who were active during the 1960s. Even among the Misties themselves, he was seen as more a forerunner than a member, someone who had helped set a particular tone but then had continued on in his own highly individualistic and idiosyncratic style. He developed his concerns as a poet early on, and he continued to pursue them throughout the dramatic ruptures and shifts of the times with a kind of obsession, giving the sense of a poet driven not so much by the changing realities of the external world as by the internal forces those realities had set in motion.

As with his contemporaries, the defining event for DuoDuo's poetic worldview was the Cultural Revolution. His views of Chinese society, of human nature, of the role of poetry and the poet can be traced to the upheavals of that time; and the Cultural Revolution serves as a sort of scrim through which almost all his work has been filtered, not only as a particular historical moment but as a paradigm for the extremes of the human condition. At the most obvious level there are the references to smoking armies and smoking guns, to bloodshed, to fear, and then the more symbolic references to winds and storms, which are almost always direct or oblique allusions to the revolution. But beyond that there is a tone throughout his work, at once plaintive and bitter, that points always to a sense of idealism gone wrong, of human corruption and evil winning out over good intentions. His is a landscape where the commonplaces of existence have undergone a nightmarish skewing, where winters go on endlessly and fruit refuses to ripen, where the physical world of ploughs and felled timber and furrowed fields has become an anatomy of human pain. Desire is thwarted or inexorably twisted away from its object; death, mainly as outrage and then, in the exile poems, also as release, is always looming. It is as if the official idealized view of reality has produced this distorted underside, this unofficial other, a sort of Goyaesque breeding of monsters beneath the sleep of ideology.

An early poem, "Honeyweek," written in 1972, shows in embryo some of the major lines along which DuoDuo's poetry would develop. The poem is a parable of love gone wrong, set out in a seven-day structure like an inverse creation myth where more is destroyed than created. The tone throughout is ironic, in itself a subversive gesture in the political climate of the time; and the subject matter, seduction and its aftermath, would have been anathema in a period when the expression of personal emotion and desire was severely discouraged. In the context of the Cultural Revolution, the poem is a biting commentary on the distortion of human relationships in the name of the ideal: by day seven, after glimpsing freedom like "a buffalo" and the ideal like "dawn," the lovers have nonetheless seen the first carnal promise of their relationship subsumed by the demands of the revolution, having become "demonstration slogans slurred together" and self-denouncing themselves as "sons and daughters of bitches," a common insult during the Cultural Revolution against people of questionable class backgrounds. The final irony is that they are left "facing the east where no sun rises" — an inversion of the usual "Let there be light" of creation myths, but also a specific allusion to the official equation of communism and of Mao with the rising sun. This mocking of the language of officialdom would have been considered tantamount to high treason at the time, had it been discovered.

In presaging some of DuoDuo's main concerns as a poet, "Honeyweek" also points toward the future development of the Misty movement. The play on the image of the rising sun, for instance, would become typical of the ways in which the Misty poets tried to subvert the heavily politicized language they'd grown up with. In DuoDuo's work, images of the sun, of daybreak, of the east recur frequently, sometimes with a very specific allusion intended. In "Summer," for example, the "downcast flowers" bemoaning a sun that has fled are a reference to the oath of the Red Ties, the group that school children belonged to under Mao, in which Mao was likened to the red sun and his followers to sunflowers forever facing him. But beyond their function as parody, such references also serve as acts of reclamation, simultaneously stripping away the received meaning of the official language while reinvesting it with poetic possibility. In DuoDuo's work as a whole, there is an ongoing interplay of sun imagery with images of the moon, of night, of shadows and dusk, which are variously associated with the poet, with desire, with all that is suppressed, but also with terror, with evil, with death. It is clear that what we are dealing with is not the simple A = B logic that is the trademark of propaganda, but rather the fluidity that is poetry — in this case where connotation and association perform not only their usual poetic function, but also serve to displace the false certainties of a language made sterile by political manipulation. The entire symbolist thrust in DuoDuo's work, the recurring images and motifs, can be seen in this context: it is as if after the apocalypse he has set out to reinvent the world, to replace what has been discredited with a different, personal mythology that includes all that was previously left out.

In "Honeyweek" there is also a nod toward the view the Misty poets would eventually take that the events of the Cultural Revolution were not anomalies but part of the broad pattern of Chinese history. The two forces contending over the fate of the lovers in "Honeyweek" are those of the revolution on one hand, and of family and tradition on the other — "those noses that sniff," those "grandfathers who live long, long lives." Each in its way conspires to reduce desire to social form, family and tradition to marriage ("You're no longer in love? / That's right; it's time to marry"), and the revolution to parades and slogans. In later poems, this sense of the continuity between oppression old and new becomes at once more nuanced and more overt. The inference — as in " 'Throughout this drunken land,' " where the emperor, clearly a reference to Mao, snores while the people suffer — is that communism is merely feudalism by another name. The predominance in DuoDuo's poetry of rural images, at first surprising in a poet who spent most of his life in Beijing, can be partly understood in this context: it was no doubt in the countryside, first when he was posted there during the Cultural Revolution and later as a reporter for the *Peasants' Daily*, that DuoDuo saw most clearly the distance between Communist rhetoric and reality. The peasants, as the archetypal figures of suffering, were supposed to have been communism's greatest beneficiaries; and yet the condition DuoDuo found them in was probably not much better than in the worst days of feudalism. His poetry can be seen as the flip side of the "progressive," heavily censored stories he would have been obliged as a journalist to write about the peasants' lot. Hence the ongoing images of "endless hardship," and more subtly the whole intimate landscape he develops of cooking fires, of furrowed earth, of "furry villages curl[ed] up so long in darkness," a landscape based in lived reality but also standing as a paradigm of the history that the Communists were to have abolished.

The other half of this equation, however, is that the people themselves have colluded in their own oppression. In " 'You are a people,' " they bear the "strokes of centuries . . . like a genteel western lady as she / dabs away a sigh with her handkerchief." This sort of collusion creates the inevitability of suffering, where history "like a granite statue / watches the grey house fall." But DuoDuo's take on the past is not one of pure iconoclasm: if history is oppressive it is also inescapable, what makes home, home. "I belong here," the narrator in "Northern Earth" says, in "a country where a stone king / stands tall with his back to the sun, / in a big threshing ground, / in an empty classroom during vacation, / before the snow sets out from the depths of the sky." The northern earth of the poem is exactly the China of DuoDuo's work as a whole, and despite its oppressions, the "gloomy ancestral faces," "the foreheads of those failed wheat fields," there is no escaping its role in his own formation. One of the most lyrical poems in this collection, "The Climb to the View," manages to capture with great subtlety this sense of history as both burden and treasure in the image of the sun setting over a festival. Images of violence — the "red ocean storm" of sunset, the lantern shade that catches fire — are contained and subsumed in the poem by an overarching mood of serenity, in the midst of which sits history like a great brooding Buddha. There is a sense here that history, like the natural world to which it is both opposed and inextricably linked, is finally calming in its vastness — a sort of gigantic, never-finished task, but one which brings the respite, at least, of the "tiredness at day's end."

"The Climb to the View" actually shares its title with a poem by the eighth-century poet Du Fu. Like many writers of his time, Du Fu, a devout Confucianist, lived a life of sober dedication to government service. But he is often contrasted to his contemporary, Li Po, who was exiled for his alleged role in the An Lushan Rebellion and who reportedly died while drunkenly trying to embrace a watery reflection of the moon. In terms of his relationship to the state, DuoDuo comes more in the tradition of a Li Po than a Du Fu; and yet there is a consciousness in his work of a tie that has been cut, of being engaged in a project that has lost its traditional place within the social structure. "Honeyweek" wryly condemns the poet as bastard, "Winter Night Woman" as one who persists "in the madness / of arranging the stripes / on the tiger's back"; "Poet" gives a portrait of a "wimp-emperor" who succumbs "to words like bees," achieving nothing. Whatever irony is intended in such statements, they have to be read also as part of a genuine struggle. In a society with little tradition of the dissident writer, and where the emphasis had always been on making a contribution to the greater good, to scribble one's private poems in obscurity often must have seemed a futile if not downright delinquent activity. It is a testament to DuoDuo's own faithfulness to his work that he turns this dilemma from weakness into strength, acknowledging it but still persevering in a poetry that, while never shying from the political, remains always true to the more sinewy, more complex, more human demands of the poetic.

The two modern poets to whom DuoDuo makes specific reference in this collection are Marina Tsvetaeva and Sylvia Plath. There is a clear affinity between the work of these poets and that of DuoDuo: in all three we get the same sense of a writing that is intensely personal and unmediated, as if it has come directly from the unconscious to the page. But it is the comparison with Tsvetaeva that is particularly revealing. Like DuoDuo, Tsvetaeva was constantly confronting the dilemma of being a personal poet in political times, condemned both by the Soviets and, in exile, by the Russian Emigration for her refusal to conform to an unambiguous political stance. What emerges in her work is a landscape of suffering not so different from DuoDuo's, where what is large, sacred, eternal is in constant danger of being eclipsed by the human world's petty evils.

There is something of the modernist notions of alienation and dehumanization in such a thematic, and certainly DuoDuo, like the other Misty poets, was influenced by the modernists in both subject and form in the early stages of his career. But if the modernists were an early influence, in his work as a whole we see a ranging across a broad spectrum of poetic tradition: there are the echoes of classical Chinese poetry in works like "The Climb to the View" and "Silkworm: Textile"; there are the influences of romanticism, in his privileging of the individual and of self-expression, and in his use of nature as both the scarred victim of human insensitivity and as the force that subsumes the human world; there are the symbolist influences, both in the personalized iconography he develops over the course of his work and in the implication throughout that true reality is to be suggested, not named; there is his obvious predilection for the surreal, the dream-like and often nightmarish quality that informs so much of his imagery. But more than by movements, DuoDuo has been drawn by particular poets: by Plath and Tsvetaeva, by Baudelaire and Walt Whitman and Emily Dickinson, by Lorca, Neruda, Rilke, by Wallace Stevens, John Ashbery, Mark Strand. For a writer who came out of the barrenness of the Cultural Revolution, DuoDuo is surprisingly well read, partly thanks to his access, first through family and friends and then through work connections, to "internal circulation" materials not available to the general public; and his attachment to poets rather than to the idea of poetry helps explain why it is difficult to reduce his work to the tenets of a particular movement. It also helps explain how he has been able to remain true to the specificity of his own time and place, and of Chinese history and tradition, while writing in an idiom clearly situated within the wider tradition of world literature as a whole.

The opening section of this collection presents twenty-two of DuoDuo's poems in exile, many never before published in English. It is striking how the exile from which these poems take their shape is prefigured in DuoDuo's earlier work, quite explicitly as far back as 1973, in the poem "Night," but also throughout his work in the twin motif of the "unfamiliar path" leading forward and of memory pulling back. It is almost as if his earlier poems were written in retrospect, like a fiction where the end has been carefully fore-shadowed by the beginning. The closing lines of "Milestones," written four years before he left China, could stand as the epigraph to his poems in exile: "Heavy northern snow is your road, / the flesh on your shoulders is your food. / You, a traveller never glancing back, / nothing you despise will ever vanish."

It is this sense of being at once cut off from and trapped by the past that comes to dominate DuoDuo's poems in exile, in a sort of tyranny where the thing one has fled is also what one is inexorably drawn back to, like the moth to the flame in "Together." The landscape here is one where images of the present, of London, of Amsterdam, of Scotland, dissolve into those of the past as if reality has become unfixed, has ceased to be anything more than the dreamy projection of the mind. Against the stubborn "I belong here" of "Northern Earth" we have not so much an opposing "I don't belong here" as the sense that there is no longer a "here" to belong to. We are now in a world where "land sprawls void of measure, / rail lines speed in no direction," and the only thing that furthers is "fiction." The poet, in such a world, has only the treachery of words to fall back on: they are all that is left, and yet every word, as in "Only One Is Allowed," "is a bird with its head dashed to bits." There is an incantatory quality to some of the poems in this section, most notably in the repeated "surely" of "Watching the Sea" and the "is as before" of "Is as Before," that makes them read like acts of conjuring, the insistent, desperate attempt to evoke a reality that is irretrievably lost.

What one seems to find in these poems, then, is that the experience of exile has brought DuoDuo face to face with the postmodern dilemma: words have been severed from their objects, and yet there is no platform outside of words on which to stand. But while it may be difficult, even impossible, to speak meaningfully in such circumstances, the attempt must be made; and if exile is a sort of *mise en abyme*, a perpetual displacement from the object, it is also a real condition brought about by real forces, forces that have themselves held onto their power exactly by reducing words to their barest denotations and then finally separating them from lived reality. In this context, the "bird with its head dashed to bits" is part of the same process of trying to reduce experience to singularities, of trying to fit the ocean in "a smashed earthen pot"; and even if the primary experience of exile is a sort of impotence, DuoDuo is again able to acknowledge the dilemma without capitulating to it, doubting words yet still trying to give some shape through them to his situation. "Never Make Dreams," reads the title of the last poem in this section, in a sort of caution against hope; and yet the poem's final injunction is to make "what is not found in the present order."

Since he left China in 1989, DuoDuo has lived in a half-dozen countries and travelled through at least a dozen more. Though he was at one point granted landed immigrant status in Canada, that status was eventually revoked because, in his quests for work, he was often forced to remain outside Canada longer than immigration rules allow. He now makes his home in the Netherlands, where he was recently granted citizenship, and cobbles his living together from his writing and from speaking engagements and various writer-in-residencies throughout Europe and North America.

In the fall of 1997, travelling on his Dutch passport, DuoDuo was finally allowed to return to China to visit his ailing father, on the condition that he not engage in any political activity and that his visit not coincide with the annual Party Congress in Beijing. He found a China much changed from the one he had left eight years before, where the quest for material prosperity has completely overshadowed the struggle for human rights, the leadership seeming to have traded off its increasingly liberal economic policy for its continued control over any form of opposition or free expression. After eight years in the West DuoDuo could not imagine returning to the stifling atmosphere he found in the country, and so he continues to await the more definitive change that might allow him to go home for good.

It seems customary when discussing a writer from one culture before an audience from another to close by insisting on that writer's universality, this even in an age where the term "universal" has become a bit of a dirty word. In some ways that insistence is merely a way of stating the obvious, that we all live, breathe, experience beauty, feel pain, or that what we expect in literature is exactly that it do its job, give us in the tiny and the specific some larger sense of what it means to be human. But clearly there is the case to be made for what is different, unfamiliar, outside our experience; and to try to level a work to its universals is to risk glossing over exactly the strangeness that might be its greatest asset, that fleeting glimpse into a world that can perhaps be felt but not quite comprehended, that moment's sense that there are terms of reference one knows nothing about. In providing some context for DuoDuo's work, my intention has been not to explain away that strangeness, but rather simply to point in what direction it might lead; and perhaps the only appropriate ending here is an apology for whatever misreadings and Western biases I have brought to that attempt. Many readers will have come to DuoDuo's work with their own different insights about the context from which it has arisen; for the rest, I hope I have provided a useful footnote, at least, for what is the important thing, the poetry itself.

Nino Ricci

ACKNOWLEDGEMENTS

I am deeply indebted to so many people who were of immense help to me during the writing of this book. My first thanks must go to DuoDuo for his commitment to this book and his assistance with it. I also thank John Fraser for initiating this project. My utmost gratitude goes to Yu Li Ming and Hu Huainian for their literal translations of DuoDuo's poems which formed the basis of this book. I thank Cellan Jay for connecting me with Yu Li Ming, and Yu Li Ming for his always insightful and diligent efforts during the many hours we worked together. I acknowledge our indebtedness to the other translators of DuoDuo whom we consulted: Gregory Lee, John Cayley, Maghiel van Crevel, Jin Zhong sometimes with Steven Haven, Donald Finkel, Tang Chao, Michelle Yeh, Tony Barnstone with Newton Liu, John Rosenwald, and Yun Wang.

I greatly thank my editors, Steven Heighton and Victor Coleman, for their invaluable comments, criticisms and guidance, and their direct contributions to this book. I'm deeply grateful to Martha Sharpe, editor at Anansi, for her unflagging commitment to this project from when it was barely commenced and through many delays, as well as for her unfailing grace and good counsel, and her skilful copyediting. I also thank Michael Byron Davis and the Anansi editorial board. As well, I am very grateful to Nino Ricci for undertaking his afterword to this book.

Some of these poems have appeared in *Brick* and *Poetry Canada*.

I thank Maghiel van Crevel for providing some relevant materials, including his PhD thesis on DuoDuo, published in English in the Netherlands. I'm also grateful to Alice de Jong and Arjan Roos for their assistance. I thank Tim Wilson for summarily transporting me into this business of contemporary Chinese poetry translation with a previous project for Mangajin Books of Toronto. I'm grateful to Tim Lilburn for his interest in this project, and his encouragement over these years. Finally, I deeply thank Nino Ricci and my parents, Merle and Roy Robinson, for their support on all levels during the time I was working on this book.

Yu Li Ming thanks his wife, Ling Li Bin, for her support, and his daughter, Yu Jing Wei, for her great interest.

For help with his afterword, Nino Ricci is grateful to Tony Barnstone's Introduction to *Out of the Howling Storm: The New Chinese Poetry* (Hanover, New Hampshire: Wesleyan University Press, 1993); Lee Ou-fan Lee's "Beyond Realism: Thoughts on Modernist Experiments in Contemporary Chinese Writing," in *Worlds Apart: Recent Chinese Writing and Its Audiences*, edited by Howard Goldblatt (Armonk, New York: M.E. Sharpe, Inc., 1990); William Tay's "'Obscure Poetry': A Controversy in Post-Mao China," and Pan Yuan and Pan Jie's "The Non-Official Magazine *Today* and the Younger Generation's Ideals for a New Literature," both in *After Mao: Chinese Literature and Society, 1971–1981*, edited by Jeffrey C. Kingley (Cambridge: Harvard University, 1985); and Xiaomei Chen's "'Misunderstanding' Western Modernism: The *Menglong* Movement in Post-Mao China," in *Representations* 35 (Summer 1991). Nino Ricci is also deeply grateful to Lee Robinson for her incisive insights on DuoDuo's poetry and poetics, to Yu Li Ming for his extensive comments on Chinese history and culture, and, of course, to DuoDuo.

Thanks are also due to PEN Canada for their committed assistance to DuoDuo during his several tenures in Canada, as well as to the Canada Council for the Arts for its assistance to DuoDuo.